P9-AQN-286

A Gift For
Claire
FROM
Gigi, for us
to read!

Bedtime Stories

A Collection of Calming Classics

HarperCollins*Publishers*

BOK 1004

Published under license from HarperCollins Publishers Inc.
© 1944 Western Publishing Company, Inc.
Copyright renewed 1972. All rights reserved.
ISBN 0-06-025065-8
Printed in China.

Contents

Contents

1

Little Red Riding Hood

Once upon a time, in a cottage at the edge of a deep woods, lived a little girl and her mother. The little girl always wore a little red cape her grandmother had made for her, with a red hood to cover her curls. So the neighbors called her Little Red Ridinghood.

One morning Red Ridinghood's mother put a loaf of crusty brown bread, some spiced meat, and a bottle of red wine into a basket and said to her, "I want you to take these goodies to your grandmother, who is sick. But be sure to go straight along the woods path, and do not stop to play or talk to any strangers."

Little Red Ridinghood promised to be careful. She put on her little cape and hood, took the little basket, and off she started. She loved the walk through the shady green woods where all the flowers and birds and little animals lived. But today she did not stop to play with any of her forest friends. She kept right on the path.

Suddenly from behind a big oak tree a great gray wolf appeared. He was an evil-looking fellow, but he smiled at Little Red Ridinghood, and said politely:

"Good morning, my dear. And where are you going this fine day?"

"My grandmother is sick and I am going to her little cottage in the woods, to take her this basket from my mother. And my mother says I am not to stop to play along the way or speak to strangers."

"Always obey your mother, my dear," said the wolf, eyeing Little Red Ridinghood hungrily. "Now I do not want to delay you, since you have a long way to go, so good day!"

With a little bow the wolf disappeared among the trees, and Red Ridinghood skipped along toward her grandmother's house.

The wicked wolf, meanwhile, had taken a short cut through the woods, and he reached the grandmother's cottage long before Little Red Ridinghood.

"Who is there?" called the grandmother, who was still in bed.

"It is I, Little Red Ridinghood," said the wolf, trying to make his voice sound soft and sweet.

"Come in, my dear," said the grandmother. "Just pull the latchstring."

So the wolf pulled the latchstring and

slipped into the grandmother's cottage, and he ate her up in one big bite. Then he put on her nightgown and nightcap and climbed into her bed. He was just pulling the sheet up over his nose when Little Red Ridinghood rapped at the door.

"Who is there?" called the wolf, trying to make his voice sweet and quavery. "It is I, Little Red Ridinghood," said the little girl.

"Come in, my dear," said the wolf. "Just pull the latchstring."

So Red Ridinghood went in and put her little basket down on the table.

"Now come closer, my dear," said the wolf.

"Why, Granny, what big ears you have!" cried Little Red Ridinghood, walking closer.

"The better to hear you with, my dear," said the wolf.

"And Granny, what big eyes you have!" cried Little Red Ridinghood.

"The better to see you with, my dear," said the wolf.

"And Granny, what big teeth you have!"

"The better to EAT you with!" snapped the wolf, springing at Little Red Ridinghood. Calling for help, she ran out of the cottage and straight into the arms of a sturdy woodcutter.

He stepped into the cottage, and with one blow of his axe killed the wicked wolf. He cut him open, and out stepped Little Red Ridinghood's grandmother, none the worse for her fright.

She kissed Little Red Ridinghood warmly, and thanked the woodcutter for saving their lives. Then, after they all had a nice lunch from the goodies in Little Red Ridinghood's basket, the woodcutter took the little girl home.

There has never been another wolf seen in that forest, but Little Red Ridinghood takes no chances. She keeps right on the path, does not stop to play along the way, and never speaks to strangers.

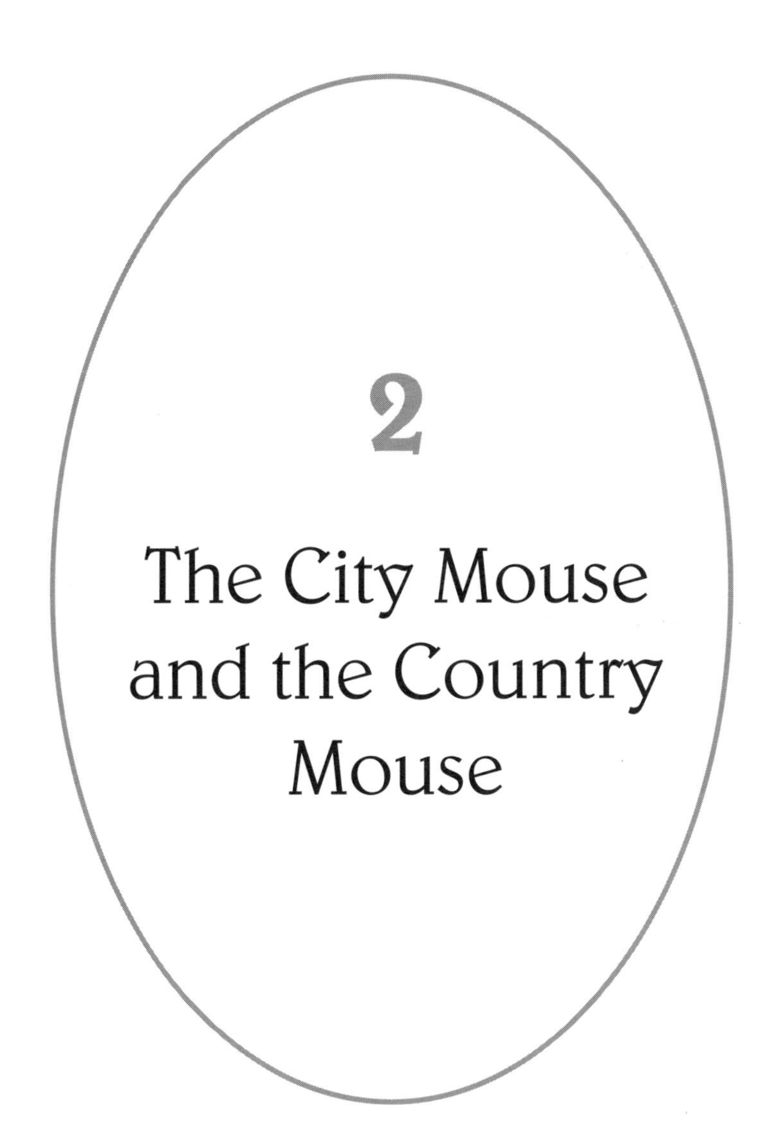

2

The City Mouse and the Country Mouse

There was once a happy little Country Mouse, who lived in a big wheat field. In the summer she feasted on grains of wheat or on bits of bread from the farmers' lunch boxes. When the weather grew cold she moved into the farmhouse and picked up bits of cake and bread and cheese which the cook dropped on the kitchen floor. These she stored away in her little mouse hole in the attic until she had a good supply laid in for the winter.

Now one day during the winter the little Country Mouse's cousin, a City Mouse, came to visit her. When they had chatted for a while, the little Country Mouse took her visitor to see her attic pantry. Proudly she showed her the mound of cheese bits, the heaps of bread and cake crumbs, and the neat piles of nuts and dried peas.

But when the City Mouse had eaten a hearty dinner, she wiped her whiskers daintily and said,

"You poor thing! So this is the way you live, on left-overs dried up in the attic. Come with me to the city and I will show you a real feast!"

The Country Mouse immediately felt rather ashamed of her simple home, so she quietly went along with the City Mouse to visit her.

The City Mouse led the way into a huge brick house, up a great staircase, and into a dining room.

The rich people who lived in the big house with the City Mouse were just having dinner, so the two little mice hid behind the door.

"Keep very still," said the City Mouse. "When they leave the table we can have all the food that is left."

The eyes of the little Country Mouse grew big and round at that, for she had never seen so much food in her whole busy life. So she sat very still until, with a scuffling of feet and scraping of chairs, the big people left the table.

"Come on," squeaked the City Mouse. Peeking cautiously to right and left she led the way across the room, up onto a chair, and from the chair onto the table, with the Country Mouse scampering along behind her.

The Country Mouse took a long look around her at the table still crowded with good things, and sighed a deep, happy sigh.

"This is wonderful," she said, taking a big bite out of a beautiful cheese. "You live just like a prince!"

She had scarcely finished squeaking when, with a snarl, a cat pounced up on the table. After her came the cook, shouting and waving a big spoon. And into the room bounded two dogs, barking fiercely. Then there was a terrible row! In the midst of it the two mice skittered down to the floor and dodged into a handy hole.

"We'll wait until all is quiet again and go back for some more," whispered the City Mouse.

But her country cousin shook her head firmly.

"We'll wait until it is quiet again and then I'll go home as fast as I can. You are welcome to all the fine food you can get, my friend. As for me, I prefer my dry crusts in my peaceful attic!"

3

The Gingerbread Boy

Once upon a time there lived a little old man with his little old wife in a little old house in the woods. They were very happy, but they had no children and they did want a little boy of their own.

One morning when the little old woman was baking gingerbread she chuckled to herself and said, "I'll make my little old man a gingerbread boy."

So she took a piece of spicy dough, and she rolled it out smooth, and she cut it out in the shape of a fine gingerbread boy. She gave him raisins for eyes, and a wide smiling mouth, and down the front of his jacket she put a row of currant buttons. Then, with a little pat, she popped him into the hot oven.

When she thought the gingerbread boy should be baked clean through, the little old woman, still chuckling to herself, opened the door to peek in. But before she had time to put a finger on him, the gingerbread boy hopped right out of the oven, skipped through the kitchen door, and ran down the path to the woods.

The little old woman ran after him, calling, "Come back, come back!" But the gingerbread boy only laughed and cried out:

"Run, run as fast as you can,
You can't catch me,
I'm the gingerbread man.

He was right. The little old woman could not catch him.

The little old man saw the gingerbread boy run past with the little old woman after him.

"Come back, come back!" he called.

But the gingerbread boy only laughed and cried out:

"Run, run as fast as you can,
You can't catch me,
I'm the gingerbread man.
I've run away from the little old woman
And I can run away from you, too,
I can, I can."

Then into the woods he dashed.

A plump bunny nibbling greens at the edge of the woods looked up as the gingerbread man ran past, and his bunny nose quivered hungrily.

"Come back, come back," he called.

But the gingerbread boy only laughed and cried out:

"Run, run as fast as you can,
You can't catch me,
I'm the gingerbread man.
I've run away from the little old woman
And the little old man
And I can run away from you, too,
I can, I can."

The bunny hopped along as fast as he could, but he could not catch him either, so the gingerbread boy ran on deeper into the woods.

A fuzzy bear cub sniffing for honey looked up as he passed, and his little red tongue flipped out hungrily.

"Come back, come back," he called.

But the gingerbread boy only laughed and cried out:

"Run, run as fast as you can,
You can't catch me,
I'm the gingerbread man.
I've run away from the little old woman
And the little old man

And the bunny
And I can run away from you, too,
I can, I can."

The bear cub scrambled along as fast as he could, but he could not catch him. So the gingerbread boy ran on into the deep woods.

A fox peeked out of hiding as he passed, and his sharp eyes shone hungrily.

"Watch out, gingerbread boy," he called.

The gingerbread boy only laughed and cried out:

"Run, run as fast as you can,
You can't catch me,
I'm the gingerbread man.
I've run away from the little old woman
And the little old man
And the bunny
And the bear cub
And I can run away from you, too,
I can, I can."

But the fox did not run after him. He just said sweetly, "I don't want to catch you, gingerbread boy. But there is a river just ahead, and I will give you a ride across on my tail if you like, so that the little old woman and the little old man and the plump bunny and the fuzzy bear cub will not be able to catch you."

The gingerbread boy looked at the river ahead. He looked at the woods behind. Then he looked at the fox.

"Kind fox, since your tail is so far from your mouth I will accept the ride," he decided.

So he hopped onto the fox's tail and the fox started across the river. As the water grew deeper he called to the gingerbread boy:

"Hop on my back or you will get wet."

So the gingerbread boy hopped up onto the fox's back, and on they went. Then the water got still deeper and the fox called out:

"Hop up on my head or you will get wet."

So the gingerbread boy hopped up onto the fox's head. Suddenly the sly fox flipped his head and opened his mouth and in popped the gingerbread boy.

And that was the end of that gingerbread boy.

4

The Foolish Milkmaid

One day a milkmaid was walking along, carrying a jar of milk on her head. As she went she thought:

"With the money I earn from selling this milk I shall buy some eggs. Then I shall have three hundred eggs. From those I should get at least two hundred and fifty baby chicks. When the chickens are old enough I shall sell them in the market and with the money they bring I shall buy a new dress. It will be—let's see, I think blue is my most becoming color, so it will be blue. I'll wear my new dress to the fair and I shall look so beautiful that all the young men will be begging for a dance with me. But I shall just toss my head and walk away!"

As she thought about it, she tossed her head proudly, and down in the dust rolled the jar from her head, spilling milk all around. And away flew all her fine dreams.

It never pays to count your chickens before they are hatched!

Turn the page for
more stories.

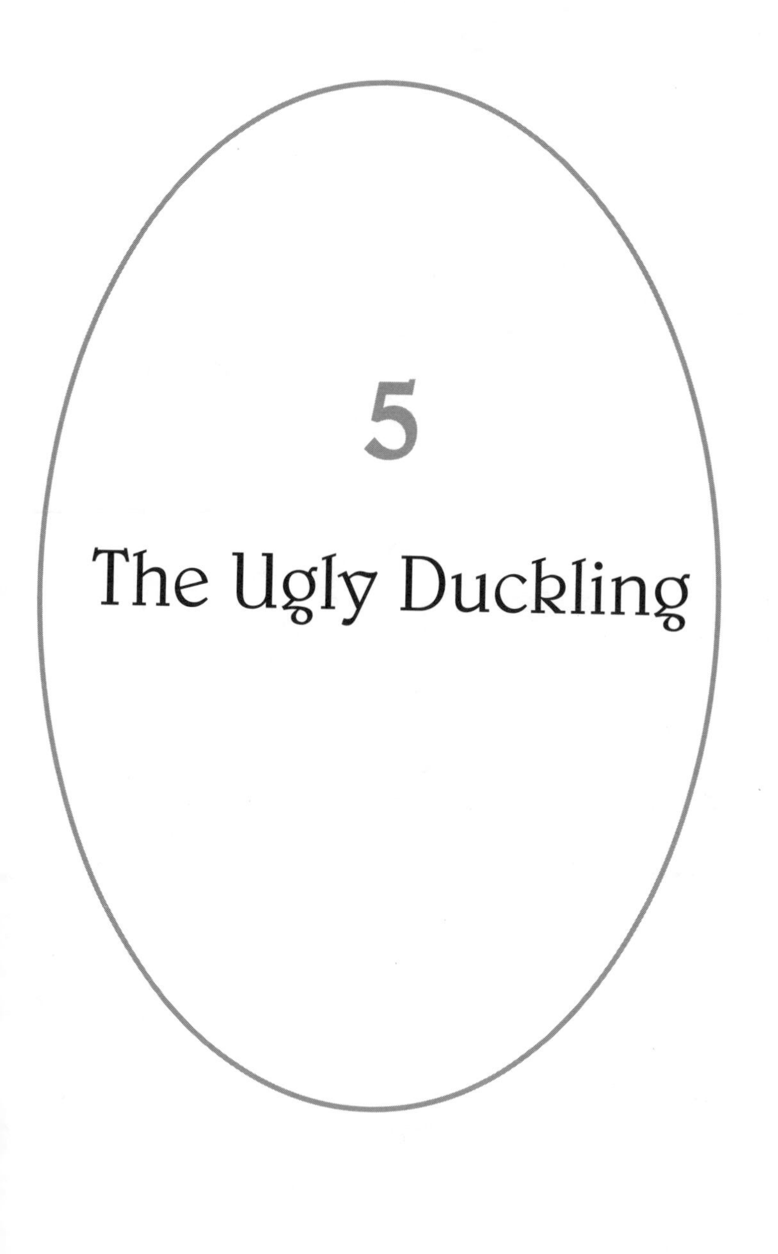

5

The Ugly Duckling

The country was lovely; it was summer. In the shade of great leaves which formed a secluded shelter near a farmhouse, a duck was sitting on her nest. Her little ducklings were just about to be hatched, but she was nearly tired of sitting, for it had lasted a long time.

At last one egg after another began to crack. "Cheep, cheep!" they said. All the chicks had come to life, and were poking their heads out.

"How big the world is!" said all the young ones.

"Do you imagine this is the whole world?" said the mother. "It stretches a long way on the other side of the garden, right into the parson's field. I suppose you are all here now?" and she got up. "No, I declare I have not got you all yet! The biggest egg is still there; how long is it going to last?" and then she settled herself on the nest again.

At last the big egg cracked. "Cheep, cheep!" said the young one and tumbled out; how big and ugly he was! The duck looked at him.

"That is a monstrous big duckling," she said. "None of the others looked like that; can he be a turkey chick? Well, we shall soon see if he swims."

So the mother duck with her whole family went down to the water.

Splash, into the water she sprang.

"Quack, quack!" she said, and one duckling plumped in after the other. Even the big ugly gray one swam about with them.

"No, that is no turkey," the mother duck said. "See how beautifully he uses his legs and how erect he holds himself; he is my own chick! After all, he is not so bad when you come to look at him properly."

Then they went into the duckyard.

"Use your legs," said she; "mind you quack properly, and bend your necks to the old duck over there. She is the grandest of them all."

They did as they were bid, but the other ducks round about looked at them and said, quite loud, "Just look there! Now we are to have that tribe, just as if there were not enough of us already, and, oh dear! how ugly that duckling is! We won't stand him!" and a duck flew at him at once and bit him in the neck.

"They are handsome children," said the old duck, "all good looking except this one. It's a pity you can't make him over again."

"He is not handsome," said the mother duck, "but he is a good creature, and he swims as beautifully as any of the others." She patted his neck and stroked him down. "Besides, he is a drake," said she, "so it does not matter so much. I believe he will be very strong, and I don't doubt but he will make his way in the world."

After that they felt quite at home. But the poor duckling who had been the last to come out of the shell, and who was so ugly, was bitten, pushed about, and made fun of by the ducks and the hens; and the girl who fed them kicked him aside.

Matters grew worse and worse. At last, even his mother said, "I wish to goodness you were miles away!"

So he ran off and flew right over the hedge. He ran on and on. Then he came to a great marsh where the wild ducks lived; he was so tired and miserable that he stayed there a whole night.

In the morning the wild ducks flew up to inspect their new comrade.

"What sort of creature are you?" they inquired. "You are frightfully ugly, but that does not matter to us, so long as you do not marry into our family!"

Poor fellow, he had no thought of marriage; all he wanted was permission to lie among the bushes and drink a little of the marsh water.

He stayed there two whole days. Then he hurried away from the marsh as fast as he could.

Toward night he reached a poor little cottage; it was such a miserable hovel that it could not make up its mind which way to fall, and so it remained standing. He saw that the door had fallen off one hinge and hung so crookedly that he could creep into the house through the crack, and by this means he made his way into the hut's one small room.

An old woman lived there with her cat and her hen. In the morning the strange duckling was discovered immediately, and the cat began to purr and the hen to cluck.

They let the duckling sit in the corner, but they had no use for his opinion on any subject. Soon he began to think of the fresh air and the sunshine; uncontrollable longing seized him to float on the water, and at last he could not help telling the hen about it.

"What on earth possesses you?" she asked. "You have nothing to do; that is why you get these freaks into your head. Lay some eggs or take to purring, and you will get over it."

"I think I will go out into the wide world," said the duckling.

"Oh, do so by all means," said the hen.

So away went the duckling. He floated

on the water and ducked underneath it, but he was looked at askance by every living creature for his ugliness.

Now the autumn came on. One evening, just as the sun was setting in wintry splendor, a flock of beautiful large birds appeared out of the bushes. They were dazzlingly white swans with long waving necks; uttering a peculiar cry, they spread their magnificent broad wings and flew away from the cold regions to warmer lands and open seas.

The ugly little duckling craned his neck up into the air after them. Then he uttered a shriek so piercing and so strange that he was quite frightened by it himself. Oh, he could not forget those beautiful, happy birds. He did not know what they were, but he was more drawn toward them than he had ever been to any creatures before.

The winter was so bitterly cold that the duckling was obliged to swim about in the water to keep it from freezing, but every night the hole in which he swam got smaller and smaller; at last he was so weary that he could move no more, and he froze fast into the ice.

Early in the morning a peasant came along and saw him; he hammered a hole in the ice with his heavy wooden shoe, and carried the duckling home to his wife. There he soon revived. The children wanted to play with him, but the duckling was frightened and rushed in his fright into the milk pan, and the milk spattered all over the room. Then he flew into the butter cask, and down into the meal tub and out again. Just imagine what he looked like by this time!

The woman screamed and tried to hit him with the tongs, and the children tumbled over one another trying to catch him. By good luck the door stood open, and the duckling flew out among the bushes and the new-fallen snow, and lay there exhausted.

But it would be too sad to mention all the privation and misery he had to go through during that hard winter. When the sun shone warmly again, the duckling was in the marsh, lying among the rushes.

All at once he raised his wings, and they flapped with much greater strength than before and bore him off vigorously. Before he knew where he was he found himself in a large garden with a lovely lake.

Just in front of him he saw three beautiful white swans; with rustling feathers they swam lightly over the water. The duckling recognized the majestic birds, and he was overcome by a strange melancholy.

"I will fly to them, the royal birds, and they will hack me to pieces, because I am so ugly. Better be killed by them than snapped at by ducks, and pecked at and spurned by all."

So he flew into the water and swam

toward the stately swans; they saw him and darted toward him with ruffled feathers.

"Kill me, oh, kill me!" said the poor creature, bowing his head toward the water. But what did he see reflected in the clear water?

He saw below him his own image, but he was no longer a clumsy, dark gray bird, ugly and ungainly; he was himself a swan! The big swans swam round and round him, and stroked him with their bills.

Soon little children came into the garden with corn and pieces of bread, which they threw into the water, and the smallest one cried out, "There is a new one!" And they clapped their hands and danced about.

The new swan felt quite shy, and hid his head under his wing. He thought of how he had been pursued and scorned, and now he heard them all say that he was the most beautiful of all beautiful birds. He rustled his feathers and raised his slender neck aloft, saying with exultation in his heart, "I never dreamed of so much happiness when I was the Ugly Duckling."

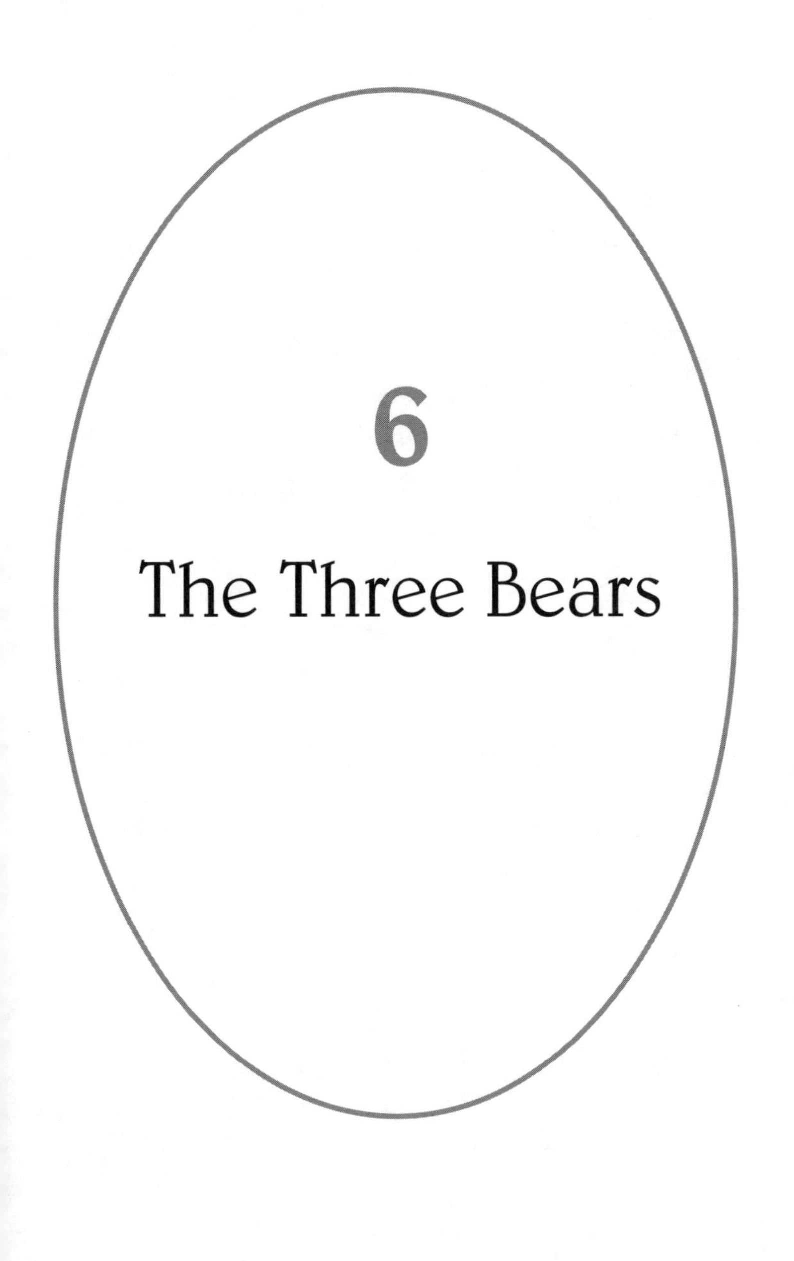

6

The Three Bears

In a neat little cottage in the midst of a deep woods there once lived three bears. One was a great big daddy bear. One was a middle-sized mother bear. And one was a wee little baby bear.

One morning Mother Bear made a big batch of porridge for breakfast. She filled a great big bowl for Daddy Bear, a middle-sized bowl for her middle-sized self, and a wee little bowl for Baby Bear.

Then they all went out for a walk in the woods while the porridge was cooling.

That same morning a little girl named Goldilocks had gone for a walk by herself. She had gone much farther than she should have and found herself in the deep woods where she had never been.

All at once she saw through the trees a neat little cottage.

"I wonder who lives there, way off in the woods," she thought.

She knocked on the door, but no one came, so she walked right in. There was no one in the living room, but it looked very comfortable, so Goldilocks decided to sit down to rest.

First she sat in the great big daddy bear chair.

"This is much too hard for me," she said.

Then she sat in the middle-sized mother bear chair.

"This is much too soft for me," she said.

Then she sat in the wee little baby bear chair.

"This is just right," she said.

But as she sat down, it broke all to pieces!

So Goldilocks went on until she found the three bowls of porridge set out to cool. It smelled very good, so she decided to taste it.

First she tasted the porridge in the great big daddy bear bowl.

"This is too hot for me," she said.

Then she tasted the porridge in the middle-sized mother bear bowl.

"This is too cold for me," she said.

Then she tasted the porridge in the wee little baby bear bowl.

"This is just right," she said, and ate it up!

Then Goldilocks went upstairs. There was no one there either, but the beds looked very inviting, so she decided to take a nap.

First she tried the great big daddy bear bed.

"This is too hard for me," she said.

Then she tried the middle-sized mother bear bed.

"This is too soft for me," she said.

Then she tried the wee little baby bear bed.

"This is just right!" she said.

So she curled up and fell asleep.

Soon the three bears came home from their walk. They could soon see that someone had been in their house.

"SOMEONE'S BEEN SITTING IN MY CHAIR," said the father bear in his great big voice.

"SOMEONE'S BEEN SITTING IN MY CHAIR," said the mother bear in her middle-sized voice.

"Someone's been sitting in my chair," said the baby bear in his wee little voice, "and has broken it all to pieces."

The three bears looked around at the bowls of porridge they had set out to cool.

"SOMEONE'S BEEN TASTING MY PORRIDGE," said the father bear in his great big voice.

"SOMEONE'S BEEN TASTING MY PORRIDGE," said the mother bear in her middle-sized voice.

"Someone's been tasting my porridge," said the baby bear in his wee little voice, "and has eaten it all up."

Now the three bears hurried upstairs

"SOMEONE'S BEEN SLEEPING IN MY BED," said the father bear in his great big voice.

"SOMEONE'S BEEN SLEEPING IN MY BED," said the mother bear in her middle-sized voice.

"Someone's been sleeping in my bed," said the baby bear in his wee little voice, "and here she is!"

Just then Goldilocks woke up. When she saw the great big father bear and the middle-sized mother bear and the wee little baby bear all standing there looking at her, she sprang out of the wee little bed, and hurried down the stairs and out of the door before the bears could turn around.

Then she ran and ran until she was home. And never again did she wander off into the deep woods alone, and never again did she see the neat little cottage of the three bears.

Turn the page for
more stories.

7

The Three Billy Goats Gruff

Once upon a time there were three Billy Goats named Gruff who lived together on a mountainside. Now on their mountainside there was very little to eat, but just across the way was a beautiful pasture of green grass. On the way to this pasture they had to pass over a bridge, and under the bridge lived a big bad troll.

One day trip-trap, the youngest Billy Goat Gruff started across the bridge.

"Who trips over my bridge?" roared the troll.

"Only Littlest Billy Goat Gruff," said the little goat in a soft voice.

"Aha! I am going to come up and eat you," said the troll.

"Oh, don't eat me," cried the Littlest Gruff. "My bigger brother is coming after me, and he is much bigger than I."

So the troll grumbled and rumbled but he let the Littlest Billy Goat Gruff cross the bridge to the pasture.

Soon TRIP-TRAP, TRIP-TRAP, the second Billy Goat Gruff started across the bridge.

"Who trips over my bridge?" roared the troll.

"ONLY MIDDLE-SIZED BILLY GOAT GRUFF," said the second goat.

"Aha! I am going to come up and eat you," said the troll.

"OH, DON'T EAT ME," cried the Middle-Sized Gruff. "MY BIGGER BROTHER IS COMING AFTER ME, AND HE IS MUCH BIGGER THAN I."

So the troll grumbled and rumbled, but he let the Middle-sized Billy Goat Gruff cross the bridge to the pasture.

Soon TRIP-TRAP, TRIP-TRAP, the biggest Billy Goat Gruff started across the bridge.

"Who tramps over my bridge?" roared the troll.

"IT IS I, GREAT BIG BILLY GOAT GRUFF," shouted the biggest goat.

"Aha! I am going to come up and eat you," said the troll.

"COME ALONG," cried Great Big Billy Goat Gruff.

So up came the old troll. But the Great Big Billy Goat Gruff put down his head and bounded forward and hurled that troll right off the bridge and he was never seen again.

Then the Great Big Billy Goat Gruff joined his brothers in the pasture. And the grass was so delicious that all three goats grew so fat that they could hardly walk home.

And snip, snap, snout, my story's out.

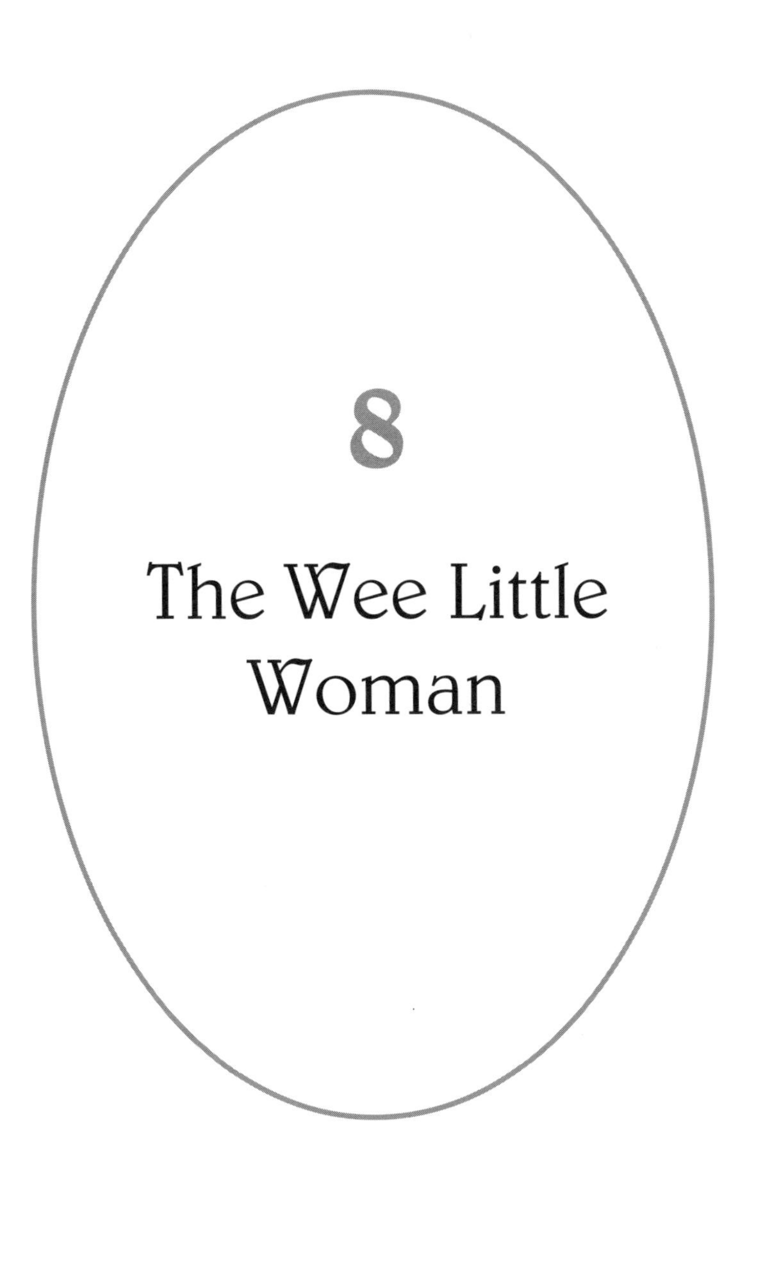

8

The Wee Little Woman

Once upon a time there was a wee little woman who lived in a wee little house in a wee little village. Now one day this wee little woman put on her wee little bonnet and went out to take a wee little walk. When she had gone a wee little way she came to a wee little market. There she saw a wee little bone.

"This wee little bone will make me a wee little soup for my wee little supper," said the wee little woman to her wee little self. So the wee little woman bought the wee little bone and took it home to her wee little house.

Now when the wee little woman got home to her wee little house she was a wee little bit tired, so she put the wee little bone in her wee little cupboard and went up her wee little stairs to her wee little bed.

When this wee little woman had been asleep a wee little time, she was awakened by a wee little voice from the wee little cupboard which said:

"Give me my bone!"

The wee little woman was a wee little bit frightened, so she hid her wee little head under the wee little covers and went to sleep again. And when she had been asleep again a wee little time, the wee little voice cried out from the wee little cupboard a wee little bit louder:

"GIVE ME MY BONE!"

This made the wee little woman a wee little bit more frightened, so she hid her wee little head a wee little way farther under the wee little covers. And when the wee little woman had been asleep again a wee little time, the wee little voice from the wee little cupboard said again, a wee little bit louder:

"GIVE ME MY BONE!"

The wee little woman was a wee little bit more frightened, but she put her wee little head out from under the wee little covers, and said in her loudest wee little voice:

"TAKE IT!

9

The Little Red Hen and the Fox

One day the Big Black Fox said to his mother, "I am hungry. What is there in the house to eat?"

"Not a bite or a sip," said Mother Fox.

"Well then," said the Big Black Fox, "put a big kettle of water on to boil. This morning I shall go after the Little Red Hen."

So off he started with a sack slung over his shoulder, in which he planned to bring back the Little Red Hen.

Now the Little Red Hen had gone out to hunt some large, juicy worms for breakfast, and she had left the door of her little house open. So when the Big Black Fox came sneaking up with his sack over his shoulder, he slipped right into the house and hid.

"Aha!" said he. "It won't be long before the Little Red Hen comes back. Then what a delicious breakfast we shall have, Mother Fox and I."

Soon the Little Red Hen came back with seven juicy worms for her breakfast. She stepped inside the house and stopped short. She knew immediately that something was wrong. But, before she could think what it was, the Big Black Fox jumped out from his hiding place.

Quicker than a wink the Little Red Hen dropped her seven juicy worms and fluttered up to the high mantel above her fireplace.

"Come down!" cried the Big Black Fox.

But the Little Red Hen was too smart for that.

"Not I," she said. "I am safer up here."

"I know a way to fix that," said the Fox, and he started to run around and around and around in a circle.

The poor Little Red Hen watched him, wondering what he was up to. And the longer she watched him circling, the dizzier she got. Finally she was so dizzy that she toppled right off the mantel.

Chuckling wickedly, the Big Black Fox stuffed her into his sack and started for home. It was a long walk and a hot day, and the Little Red Hen was a heavy load, so the Big Black Fox had to stop often to rest. Once he stopped a moment too long, and he fell sound asleep.

The Little Red Hen heard the fox begin to snore.

"This is my chance," she thought.

She reached into her apron pocket, where she kept her scissors and needle and thread. Then snip, snip, she cut a hole in the sack big enough to wriggle through.

"Now for a big stone," she said to herself.

She found one at last, just her own size. This she rolled into the sack; then she sewed up the slit she had cut.

Then off she went, lickety split, faster than she had ever gone before. She hurried back home. Once inside she closed the door behind her, locked it, and double locked it. And she locked the back door too.

About that time the Big Black Fox woke up.

"Oh dear, the water must be all boiled away by now," he said. "I must hurry home."

When he had taken just a few steps, though, he noticed how heavy his sack was.

"What a plump, juicy little hen she must be," he thought, chuckling.

When he got home, his mother was watching anxiously for him.

"You've been gone so long," she complained, "that I've had to keep adding water to keep it from all boiling away."

Sure enough, there was a great cloud of steam coming from the kettle!

"Good," said the Big Black Fox when he saw this. "Now you hold the cover off while I dump the Little Red Hen into the pot."

But, instead of the Little Red Hen, the big stone dropped with a splash into the steaming kettle, throwing boiling water all over the Big Black Fox and his mother.

That was enough for those two bad foxes! Never again did they bother the Little Red Hen in her little house in the woods.

10

Chicken Licken

One day as Chicken Licken was walking through the woods, an acorn fell on her head.

"Dear me," she thought, "the sky is falling. I must go and tell the king."

So Chicken Licken hurried off to tell the king that the sky was falling. On her way she met Henny Penny.

"Where are you going, Chicken Licken?" asked Henny Penny.

"The sky is falling and I am going to tell the king," said Chicken Licken. "You come too."

So Henny Penny and Chicken Licken hurried on together. Soon they met Cocky Locky.

"Where are you going, Chicken Licken and Henny Penny?" asked Cocky Locky.

"The sky is falling and we are going to tell the king," said Henny Penny. "You come too."

So Henny Penny and Chicken Licken and Cocky Locky hurried on, together. Soon they met Drakey Lakey.

"Where are you going, Chicken Licken and Henny Penny and Cocky Locky?" asked Drakey Lakey.

"The sky is falling and we are going to tell the king," said Cocky Locky. "You come too."

So Drakey Lakey went on with Chicken Licken and Henny Penny and Cocky Locky. Soon they met Goosey Loosey.

"Where are you going, Chicken Licken and Henny Penny and Cocky Locky and Drakey Lakey?" asked Goosey Loosey.

"The sky is falling and we are going to tell the king," said Drakey Lakey. "You come too."

So Goosey Loosey went on with Chicken Licken and Henny Penny and Cocky Locky and Drakey Lakey. Soon they met Turkey Lurkey.

"Where are you going, Chicken Licken and Henny Penny and Cocky Locky and Drakey Lakey and Goosey Loosey?" asked Turkey Lurkey

"The sky is falling and we are going to tell the king," said Goosey Loosey. "You come too."

So Turkey Lurkey went on with Chicken Licken and Henny Penny and Cocky Locky and Drakey Lakey and Goosey Loosey. Soon they met Foxy Loxy.

"Where are you going, Chicken Licken and Henny Penny and Cocky Locky and

Drakey Lakey and Goosey Loosey and Turkey Lurkey?" asked Foxy Loxy.

"The sky is falling and we are going to tell the king," said Turkey Lurkey.

"I know a shorter road to the king's palace," said Foxy Loxy. "Follow me."

So Turkey Lurkey and Goosey Loosey and Drakey Lakey and Cocky Locky and Henny Penny and Chicken Licken all followed Foxy Loxy.

But the sly old fox did not lead them to the king's palace at all. He led them straight into his hole, where he and his little ones feasted on Chicken Licken and Henny Penny and Cocky Locky and Drakey Lakey and Goosey Loosey and Turkey Lurkey.

So the king never heard that the sky had fallen on Chicken Licken. Which was probably just as well.

Turn the page for
more stories.

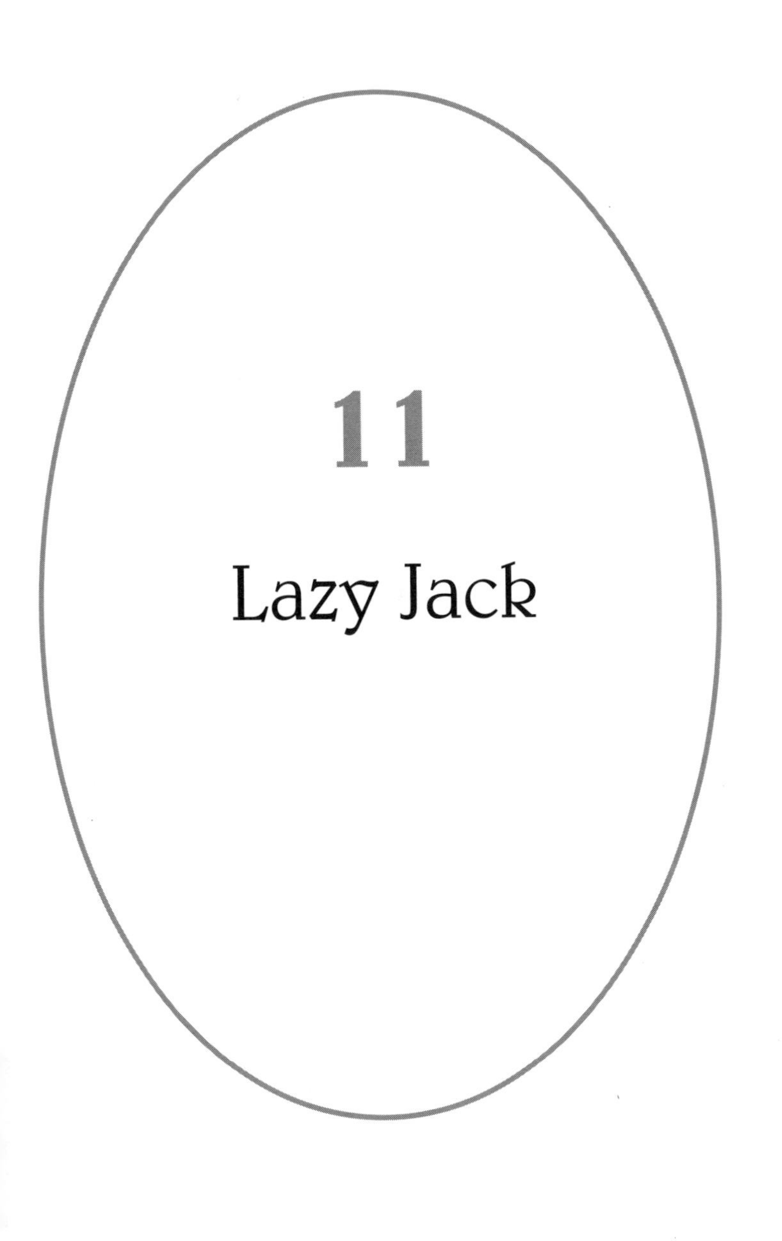

11

Lazy Jack

Once upon a time there lived in a little cottage an old woman and her son Jack. Every day the old woman sat in the corner and worked at her spinning, and every day her son sat by the fire and did nothing at all. So all the neighbors called him Lazy Jack.

One morning his mother could stand his idleness no longer, and she told Lazy Jack that he must work for his bowl of porridge. So off he went to work a day for a farmer who lived near by. At the end of the day, the farmer paid him a penny. But Lazy Jack lost the penny in the brook on his way home and had nothing to show for his work.

"The next time," said his mother, "put what you earn in your pocket."

The next day Jack worked as a cowherd for a dairyman who lived over the hill, and, at the end of the day, the farmer paid him a jug of milk.

Remembering what his mother had said, Jack tried to put the jug in his pocket. Of course he spilled all the milk and had only an empty jug when he got home.

"Next time," said his mother, "you should carry it on your head. Then you won't spill it."

The next morning Lazy Jack went once more to work for the dairy farmer. This time, when the day was over, the man gave him some cream cheese. Remembering what his mother had said, Lazy Jack put the cheese on his head and started home. But the cheese melted and ran down all over his head, and Jack had nothing to show for his day's work but a dirty face.

"Next time," said his mother patiently, "you should wrap it in green leaves and carry it in your hands."

At the end of the next day's work all Lazy Jack got was a tomcat. He did just as he had been told; he tried to wrap it in green leaves and hold it in his hands. The cat did not like this at all and finally got away from Jack, who arrived home with nothing to show but scratched hands.

"Stupid!" said his mother, who still had to spin for their living. "You should have tied it to a string and pulled it behind you."

So the next afternoon, when Lazy Jack was given a ham as payment for his work, he carefully tied a string around it and dragged it home along the dusty road.

"Oh, you strawhead!" cried his mother

when she saw the dusty, battered remains of what had been a fine ham. "Why didn't you carry it on your shoulder?"

So next day, when Jack was given a donkey for his work, he obediently hoisted it to his shoulder and started home.

Now on his way home Jack passed the handsome home of a wealthy man who had one daughter. The poor girl was both deaf and dumb, and doctors said the only cure would be for her to laugh. But, try as he might, the father could find nothing that would make his daughter laugh.

On this afternoon she was sitting at the window gazing sadly at the road. Suddenly around a bend came the strangest sight she had ever seen—Lazy Jack struggling along with the donkey on his shoulder. The donkey's four feet were waving in the air, and it was braying loudly.

First she looked. Then she stared. And then, wonder of wonders, she burst out laughing.

"Father," she called at last. "Father, look!"

"My daughter!" the old man exclaimed. "Is that really your voice I hear?"

It was, of course, and the girl was completely cured! Overjoyed, her father rushed out to the road.

"Drop your donkey," he cried to Lazy Jack. "You have given my daughter back her voice and her hearing, and no one but you shall be her husband."

So Jack, who was called Lazy Jack no longer, and the daughter were married. They lived in a fine new house and Jack's mother came to live with them. The old man came often to visit them, and, as you can well imagine, they all lived happily ever after.

12

Wolf! Wolf!

A long time ago there was a boy who watched his father's sheep. Each day he took them to a pasture on the hillside above the village, and there he sat and watched them all day long. In the afternoon, as the sun began to go down, he drove the sheep home again.

Often he would become quite lonely, because he had no one to play with. How he longed for just a little bit of company!

One day, when he was feeling very lonely indeed, he remembered what his father had told him when he first began to care for the sheep.

"You must always beware of the wolf," his father had said. "And if you should see one, be sure to call for help."

Now the boy had never seen a wolf. But he thought that it would be so pleasant to have some company that he decided to make-believe.

"Wolf! Wolf!" he cried at the top of his lungs. "Wolf! Wolf!"

Far below, the villagers heard him. They all dropped their work, seized their axes, and rushed up to the pasture. But, when they got there, they saw only the sheep and the boy. There was no wolf at all. He was so glad to see them that they were not very angry at him for having fooled them. But they told him that he must not do it again.

And for a long time he did not. One day,

though, he was feeling lonelier than ever. He knew that he should not, but he cried out, as loudly as he could,

"Wolf! Wolf!"

And again the villagers came rushing to help him. But, when they got there, they saw only the sheep and the boy, and no wolf at all. He was very glad to see them, but some of them were quite angry, this time, at having been fooled. They told him that he *must* not do it again.

And he did not. One day as he sat quietly watching his sheep, he saw a big gray wolf come slinking out of the forest.

"Wolf! Wolf!" he called with all his might. "Wolf! Wolf!"

The villagers, far below, heard his cries, but went on with their work. They did not want to be fooled again.

"Wolf! Wolf!" cried the boy. "Wolf! Wolf! Wo—"

At this the villagers were startled. Perhaps he did need help. And they dropped their work, seized their axes, and rushed to the pasture.

But they were too late. When they got there the wolf had gone, and all they ever found of the little boy was his pointed shepherd's hat.

Turn the page for
more stories.

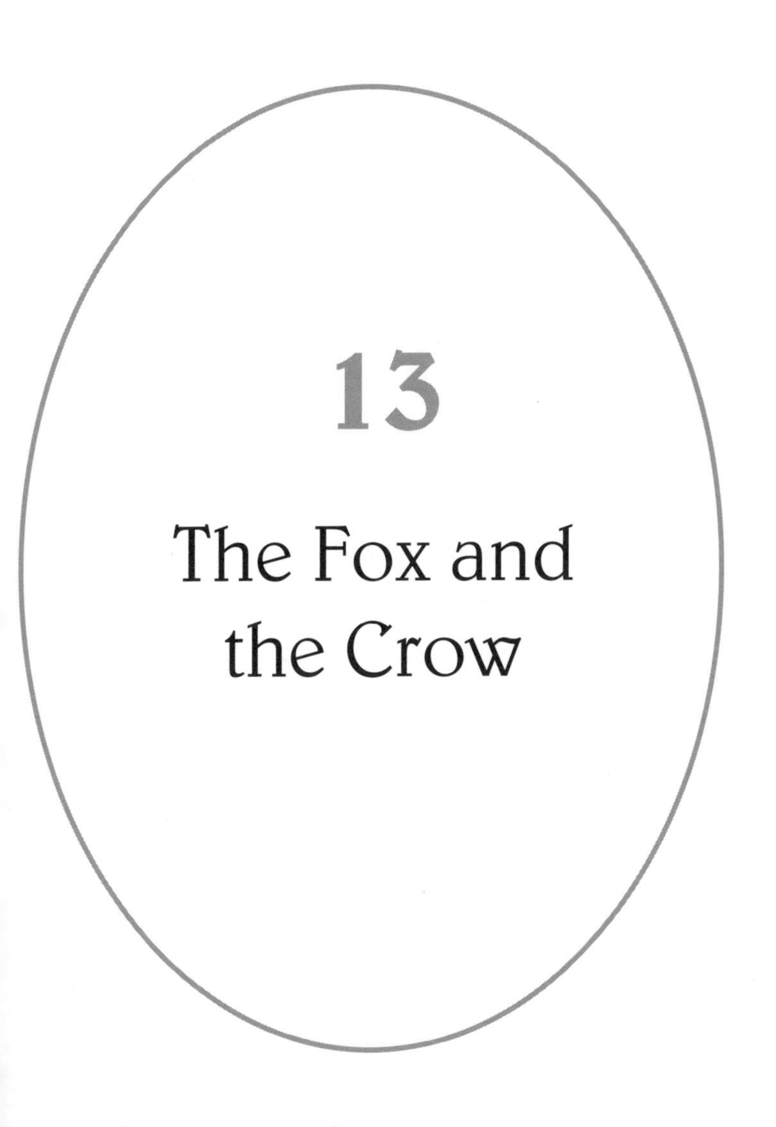

13

The Fox and the Crow

One morning a plain black crow sat on a branch holding in his beak a delicious piece of cheese.

Along came a fox, who had smelled the delicious cheese. The fox came and stood under the tree, and bowed politely to the crow.

"Good morning, my friend," said the fox. "My, how well you are looking today!"

The crow was very pleased at this, but

of course could not reply because of the cheese he held in his mouth.

"Your eyes are the most beautiful I have seen," the fox went on. "And, as for your feathers—how black and glossy they are!"

The crow was even more pleased, but still said nothing. He just sat on his branch and swelled with pride. But the fox went on.

"I have been told," he continued, "how beautifully you sing, and I should like so much to hear you! Your voice could not possibly be so lovely as your feathers, but if it were—why, you would be the most wonderful bird of the whole forest. Do sing just a few notes for me, won't you?"

This was too much for the crow. He opened his beak wide, cawed loudly, and dropped the cheese right into the mouth of the waiting fox.

"Thank you so much!" said the fox, gobbling up the cheese. "Your song was very ugly, but your cheese was delicious.

Another time, perhaps you won't be so ready to believe all the good things you hear about yourself."

And, with a wave of his tail, he trotted gaily off into the woods.

14

The Little Red Hen

Once upon a time, not so very long ago, there were a pig and a duck and a cat and a little red hen who all lived together in a cozy little house.

All day, and every day, the pig just wanted to wallow in his juicy mud puddle, the duck just wanted to swim on her little pond, and the cat just wanted to sit in the sun and wash herself with her red tongue.

This left all the work of the house for the busy little red hen.

One day as the little red hen was scratching about in the front yard, looking for a plump beetle for her dinner, she came upon a grain of wheat. That gave her an idea.

"Who will plant this grain of wheat?" she called.

"Not I," grunted the pig from his puddle.

"Not I," quacked the duck from her pond.

"Not I," purred the cat with a wide yawn.

"Very well, I will then," said the little red hen. And she did.

The grain of wheat sprouted, and it grew, and it grew until it was tall and golden and ripe.

"Who will cut the wheat?" called the little red hen.

"Not I," grunted the pig from his puddle.

"Not I," quacked the duck from her pond.

"Not I," purred the cat with a flip of her red tongue.

"Very well, I will then," said the little red hen. And she did.

Soon the grains of wheat were all ready to be ground into flour.

"Who will take the wheat to the mill?" called the little red hen.

"Not I," grunted the pig from his puddle.

"Not I," quacked the duck from her pond.

"Not I," purred the cat with a toss of her head.

"Very well, I will then," said the little red hen. And she did.

When the wheat came back from the mill, it was a little sack of fine wheat flour.

"Who will make the flour into bread?" called the little red hen.

"Not I," grunted the pig from his puddle.

"Not I," quacked the duck from her pond.

"Not I," purred the cat, stroking her whiskers.

"Very well, I will then," said the little red hen. And she did.

Soon the little red hen was taking from the oven the most beautiful crusty brown loaf of bread

"Who will eat the bread?" she called.

"I will!" grunted the pig, scrambling up from his puddle.

"I will!" quacked the duck, paddling in from her pond.

"I will!" purred the cat, with one last quick lick at her paws.

"Oh, no you won't," said the little red hen. "I found the grain of wheat. I planted the seed. I reaped the ripe grain. I took it to the mill. I baked the bread. I shall eat it myself."

And she did.

Turn the page for
more stories.

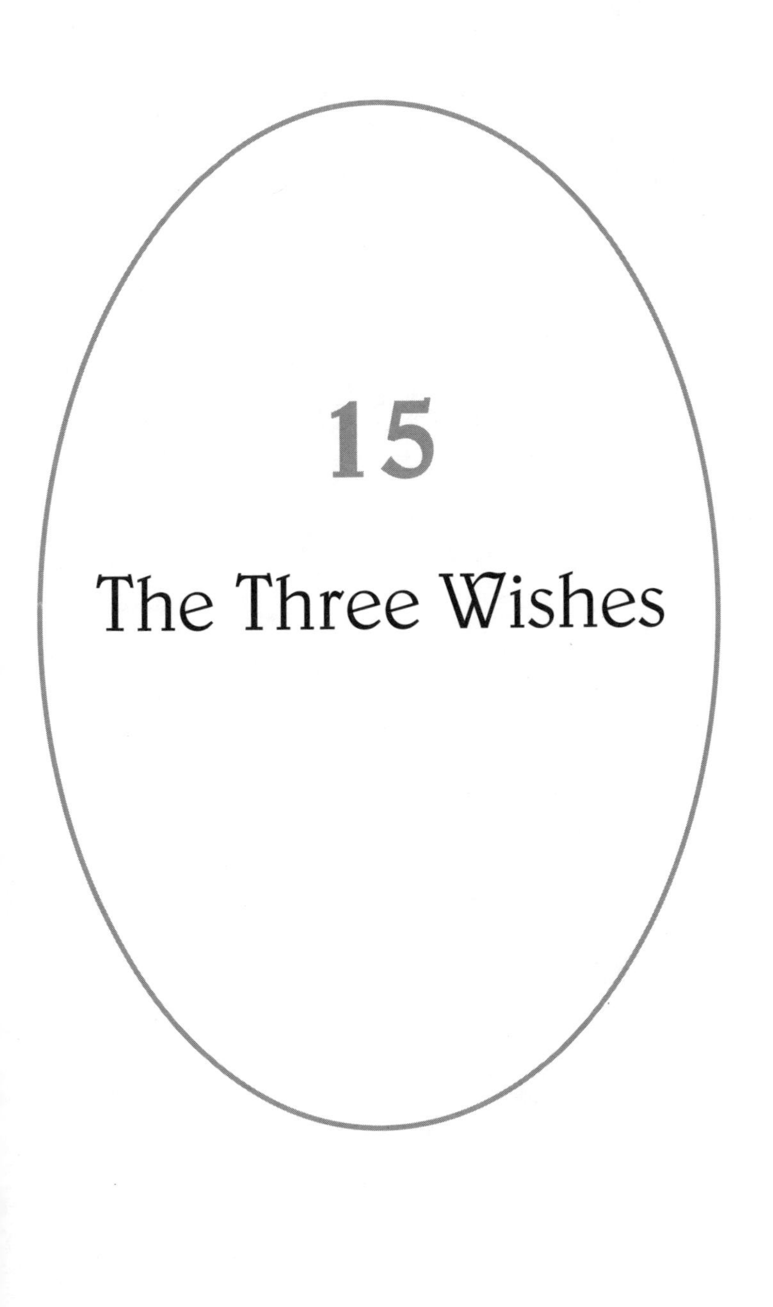

15

The Three Wishes

There once was a poor woodsman who worked hard to provide a living for himself and his wife.

One day, as he was about to cut down a fine oak tree, a small voice cried:

"Please don't cut down my tree!"

The woodsman, in great surprise, stopped and looked about him. He saw no one, so once more he lifted his axe. Just as he started to swing it, however, he heard the voice again: "Please, Mr. Woodsman, don't harm my tree!"

Again the woodsman stopped, and this time he looked very hard for the owner of the voice. But still he could find no one, and once more he raised his axe. Just then there appeared before him a little man dressed all in green.

"Don't, I beg of you, cut down my tree," said the little man. "It is my home, and if it is destroyed I shall have nowhere to live."

The woodsman, who was a kindly man, agreed, and the little man in green was so grateful that he told the woodsman that he would grant him the first three wishes he and his wife might make, whatever they were. The poor man, overjoyed at his good fortune, thanked his little friend and rushed home to tell his wife.

"Just think!" he exclaimed. "Now we

can have the cottage, the cow, and the chickens for which we have always wished.

"Stupid!" replied his wife. "If we can have whatever we like, why not wish for something far finer? I could be a queen and you a prince, and we could live in a golden castle with crystal windows."

But the man had his heart set on a pretty cottage. If he had to have a fine castle, he saw no reason why it must be of gold. And so he and his wife argued all day and far into the night about what they should wish for. The fire in the stove went out, and neither of them thought of eating. Late at night, though, the woodsman suddenly realized that he had not eaten all day.

"My, but I am hungry!" he said. "I do wish I had a bit of sausage."

And there in front of him appeared the most delicious-looking sausage you can imagine.

"Idiot!" cried his wife, almost weeping with anger. "You have used up your first wish. You and your stupid sausage!"

Now the woodsman began to lose patience.

"Oh, I wish the sausage were on the end of your nose!" he cried.

And there was the sausage, long and shiny, hanging from the end of his wife's nose.

The poor woman burst into tears of rage.

"Now your second wish is gone!" she cried.

"But we can still have your castle," said the woodcutter, half frightened at what had happened.

"Don't you dare wish for a castle!" screamed his wife. "What kind of a fine lady would I make with this sausage on my nose? You get it off!"

So the woodsman said solemnly, "I wish the sausage were off the end of my wife's nose." Instantly the sausage disappeared into thin air, and the woodcutter and his wife sat there in silence.

They had had their three wishes.

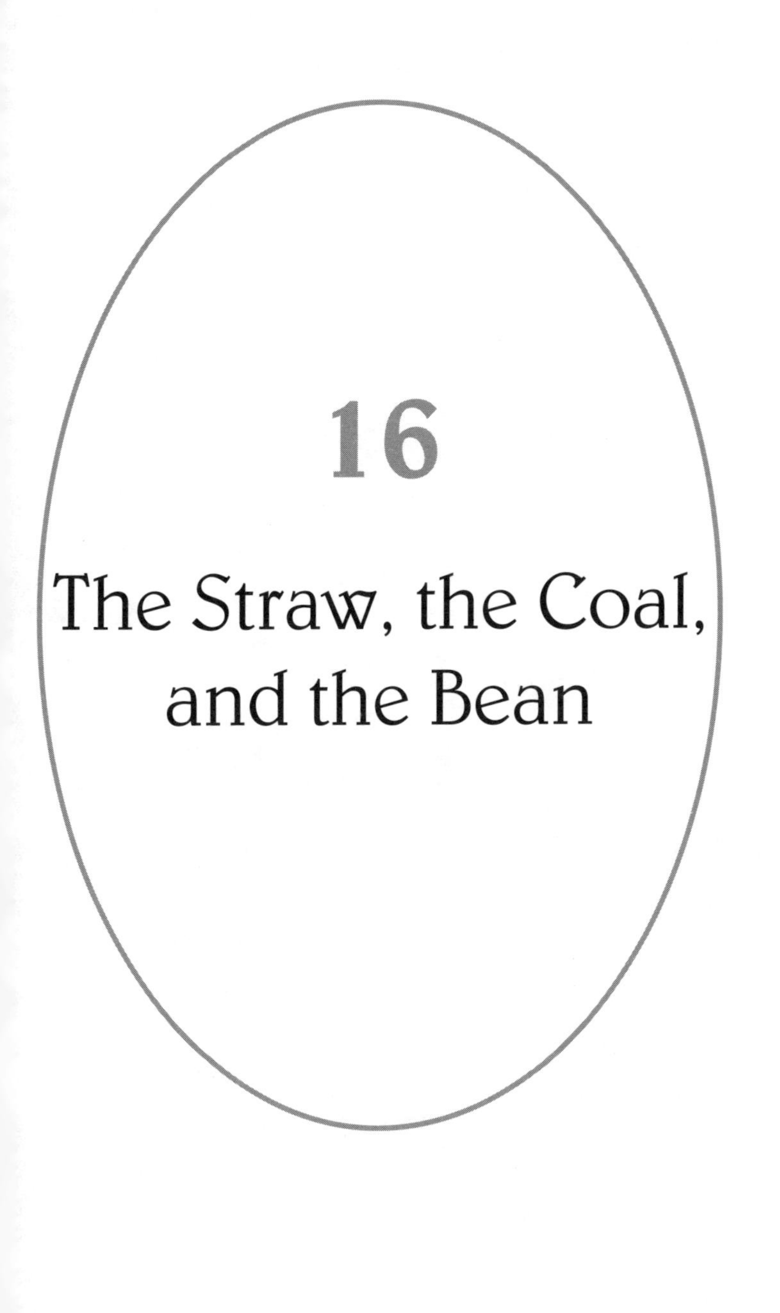

16

The Straw, the Coal, and the Bean

There was once an old woman who picked a mess of beans and made ready to cook them. She built a coal fire on her hearth, with a handful of straw to make it burn better.

When the water in the beanpot began to bubble, one of the beans popped out and fell to the hearth. Near it lay a straw, which had fallen there, and soon a red-hot coal jumped out of the fire and joined them.

The straw was the first to speak.

“How did you come here?” he asked.

“I jumped out of the fire,” answered the coal. “If I hadn’t I should certainly have been burned to ashes.”

“If the old woman had kept me in the pot,” said the bean, “I should have been cooked to pulp.”

“My fate would have been no better,” said the straw. “All my brothers have turned to fire and smoke, and I would have been with them if I had not slipped through the old woman’s fingers.”

“What shall we do now?” said the coal.

“I suggest that we go out into the world together,” answered the bean, “since we have all been so lucky as to escape with our lives.”

The others agreed to this, and all three started out together.

Soon they came to a tiny brook, without a bridge or stepping stones. They could not think how to get to the other side until the straw said:

"I will lay myself across, and you can go over me as if I were a bridge."

Then the straw stretched himself from bank to bank, and the coal trotted out on the new bridge. When he got to the center, though, the sound of the rushing water below suddenly filled him with terror, and he could not go another step. Gradually the straw got hotter and hotter, until it charred and broke in two and fell in the brook. The coal slipped down, hissing, into the water and disappeared.

The bean, which had been waiting on the bank, could not help laughing at this funny sight. It laughed and laughed until it burst. And that would have been the end of the bean, if a tailor traveling from town to town had not stopped to rest himself by the brook.

He picked up the bean, took out a stout needle and black thread, and stitched it together again. And ever since, all beans have had a black seam.

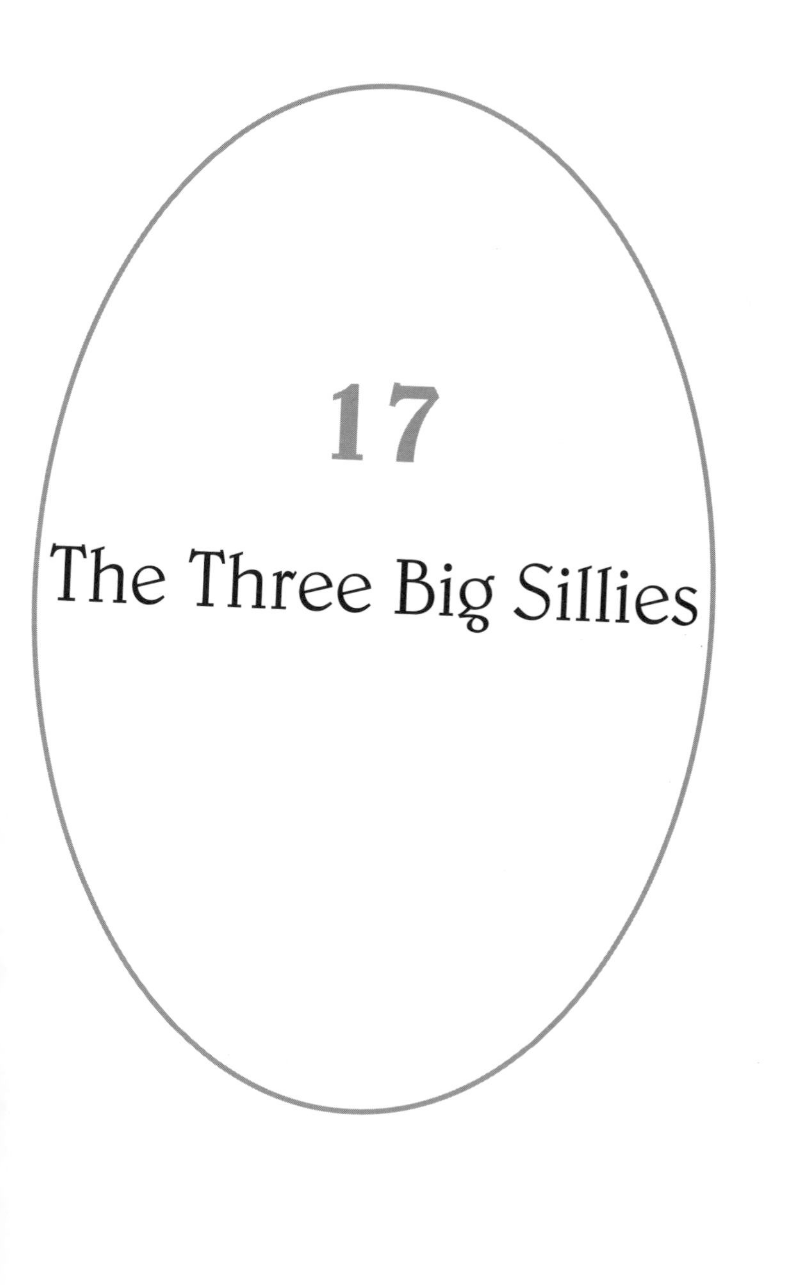

17

The Three Big Sillies

Once upon a time there were a farmer and his wife who had one daughter. A young man was courting the daughter, and he often came to have supper with the family.

One evening the young man came for supper, and the daughter went down into the cellar to bring up some eggs. While she was in the cellar she happened to notice an axe stuck in one of the beams. It must have been there a long time but she had never noticed it and it set her to thinking:

"Suppose my young man and I were married and had a son and he grew up to be a man and came down in the cellar and the axe fell on his head, and killed him, what a dreadful thing that would be!"

So she set down her candle and basket and sat herself down and started to cry.

Soon her mother began to wonder why she did not bring the eggs, so she went looking for her.

"Why are you crying, daughter?" she asked when she found the girl.

The daughter pointed to the axe in the beam and sobbed:

"Suppose my young man and I were married and had a son and he grew up to be a man and came down in the cellar and the axe fell on his head and killed him!"

"Dear, dear, what a dreadful thing that would be!" the mother agreed, and she sat down beside her daughter and began crying, too.

After a while the father began to get hungry for his supper, so he went down to see what had become of his wife and daughter.

"What ever are you crying for?" he asked when he found them.

"Suppose daughter and her young man were married and had a son and he grew up to be a man and came down in the cellar and the axe fell on his head and killed him!" said his wife.

"Dear, dear, that would be dreadful!" said the father, and he sat down beside the others and started to cry, too.

The daughter's young man, left all alone upstairs, got tired of that at last, so he went down in the cellar, too, to see what the others were doing.

"What ever is the matter?" he asked, when he saw the three of them sitting there, weeping.

"Suppose you and daughter were married and had a son and he grew up to be a man and came down in the cellar and the axe fell on his head and killed him!" said the father.

And all three began to cry louder than ever.

At that the young man burst out laughing. He just reached up and pulled down the axe, and that was that.

"I've traveled many a mile," he said, "but never have I met three such big sillies as you. Now I'm going off on my travels again, and if I meet three bigger sillies than you three, then I'll come back and marry your daughter."

So he said good-by and started off on his travels, and then the farmer and his wife and daughter sat and cried some more because the daughter had lost her young man.

The young man on his travels soon came to a little cottage with grass growing from the thatched roof. The old woman who lived there was trying to make her cow climb a ladder up to the roof, but the cow would not go.

This was a surprising thing to see, so the young man asked the old woman what she was doing.

"Why, just see all that beautiful grass on the roof," she said. "I want my cow to climb up so she can eat it. She would be safe because I'd tie a string around her neck and put it down the chimney and tie the other end around my wrist so she couldn't fall off without my knowing it."

"You big silly!" said the young man. "Why don't you cut the grass and throw it down to her?"

But the old woman was determined to do it her way, so she coaxed and pushed until she got the cow up the ladder. Then she tied a string around the cow's neck and put the string down the chimney. And she tied the other end of the string around her wrist as she went about the house.

The young man shook his head and went on his travels. But before he had gone far the cow fell off the roof and hung halfway to the ground with the string around his neck. And the cow's weight pulled the old woman half-way up the chimney, and there she stuck fast in all the soot.

So that was one big silly.

That night the young man stopped at an inn. Since it was crowded, he was given a bed in a double room. The man who had the other bed was a jolly fellow, and they spent a pleasant evening together. But next morning the young man had a surprise. For the jolly fellow hung his trousers from the knobs on the chest of drawers and ran across the room and tried to jump into them. He tried and tried and tried until he was all red and puffing, but he could not make it.

"Oh, dear," he said at last, "I do think trousers are the most awkwardest things to wear! How ever do you get into yours?"

The young man showed him, and the jolly fellow was so pleased, for he said he never would have thought of that system!

So that was another big silly.

The young man went on with his travels, and soon he came to a pond outside a little village, where all the villagers were gathered around raking at the water with pitchforks and brooms and rakes.

"What ever are you doing?" the young man asked.

"The moon has fallen into the pond!" they cried. "We're trying to rake it out!"

"Why, you big sillies!" said the young man. "The moon is still in the sky. That is only a reflection in the pond!"

But the villagers would not believe him, so the young man turned away.

And that was a lot more sillies—many more than three. So the young man went back and married the farmer's daughter.

And they lived happily ever after, I expect.

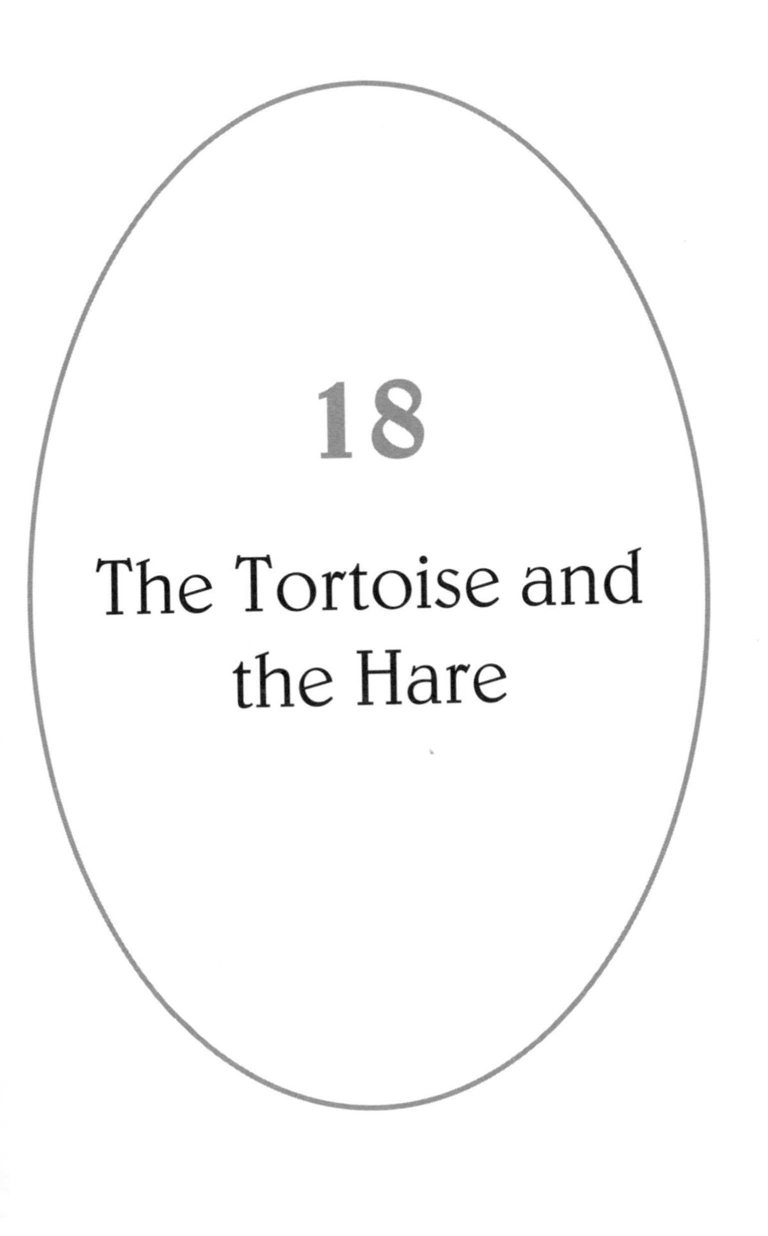

18

The Tortoise and the Hare

There was once a hare who was always boasting of his speed. "There is no one in the forest who can run as fast as I can," he told everyone, strutting up and down. "Who wants to race me?"

The other animals were tired of hearing his boasting, but no one ever offered to race him until one day the turtle spoke up.

"I will race with you," he said in his slow way.

The hare burst out laughing, and all the animals looked surprised, for everyone knew the turtle was the slowest of them all.

"Oho!" chuckled the hare. "That is a good joke. Why, I can beat you without half trying!"

"Wait until you have won before you start to boast," said the turtle.

So the race course was laid out, and all the animals gathered to see the start.

The hare bounded off in a great burst of speed that left the poor turtle far behind in the dust.

Soon the hare looked back. Finding that he could not even see the turtle coming any more, he lay down in the shade of a big tree beside the road to wait a bit, just to make the finish of the race more exciting.

But waiting made the hare sleepy, and he decided to snatch just a two-minute nap. The two minutes stretched on and on, and still the hare slept in the shade of the big tree.

All this time the turtle was plodding along the hot, dusty road. He came ever so slowly, but he kept right at it, and soon he passed the hare sleeping by the roadside.

The turtle crawled past without making a sound to wake the careless hare. When the hare finally woke up with a start, the turtle was just plodding up to the finish line, far ahead, while all the animals stood by cheering.

The hare had lost the race by being careless and cocky; he could never boast again, and all the animals were glad of that.

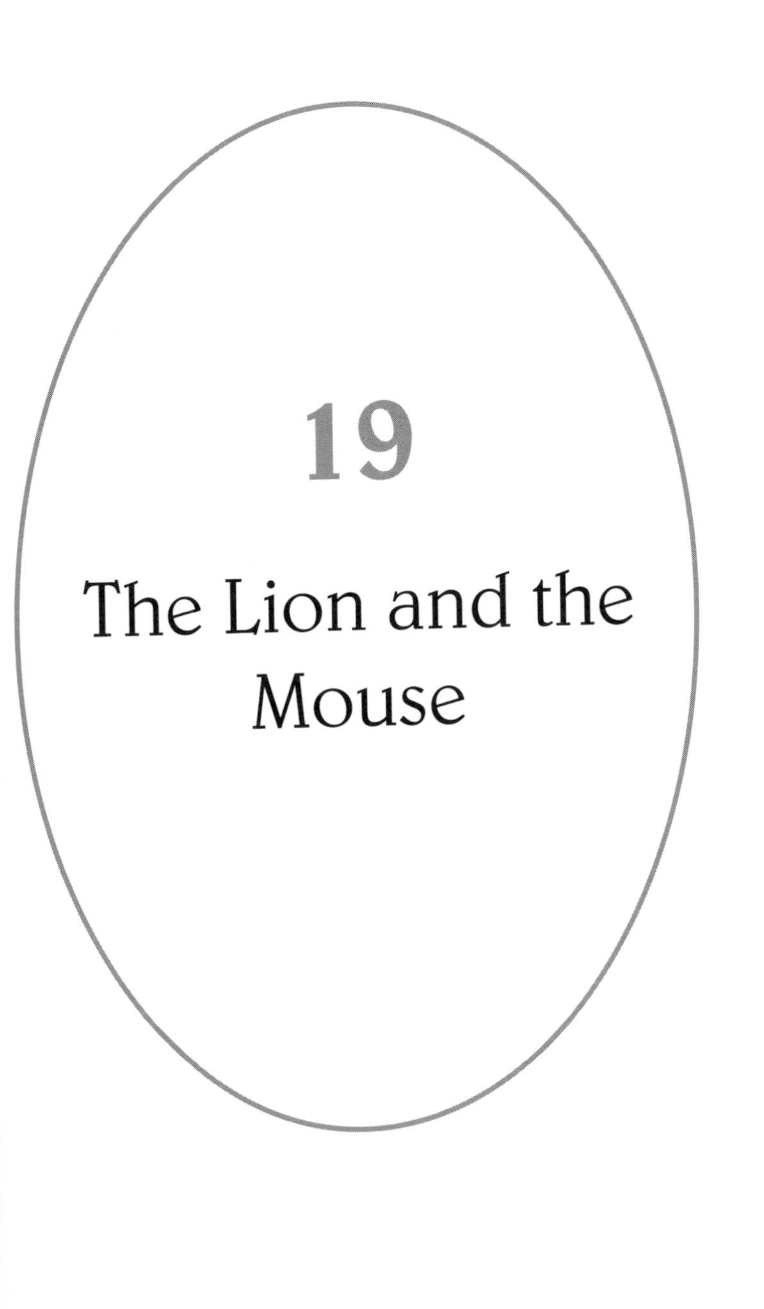

19

The Lion and the Mouse

One day, as a lion lay sleeping in his lair, a little mouse, not knowing where he was going, ran over the lion's nose.

With a roar the lion awoke, and clapped his paw over the tiny creature.

"Now I shall kill you, worthless little mouse!" thundered the lion.

"Oh, good sir," squeaked the frightened little mouse, "I meant no harm, I assure you. Nothing was further from my thoughts than to disturb your majesty! Please spare my life, for I am not even worthy of your attention."

The lion, smiling at his little prisoner's fright, lifted his paw and watched the mouse scamper away.

Months later, the lion was ranging the woods, stalking his prey, when he fell into a cunning trap made of ropes and placed there by hunters.

"I can never escape!" thought the unhappy lion, threshing about hopelessly. "Oh, woe is me!" And he set up a roar that filled the jungle with its echo.

The little mouse, scampering about his own little business, recognized the voice of the lion who had spared his life, and ran to the spot.

Without wasting a moment, the mouse set to work nibbling the ropes that held the lion. And before the hunters came to inspect their trap the lion was free.

"I thank you, good mouse," said the lion. "I see now that any kindness we can do is always worth while. I shall remember the lesson you have taught me!"

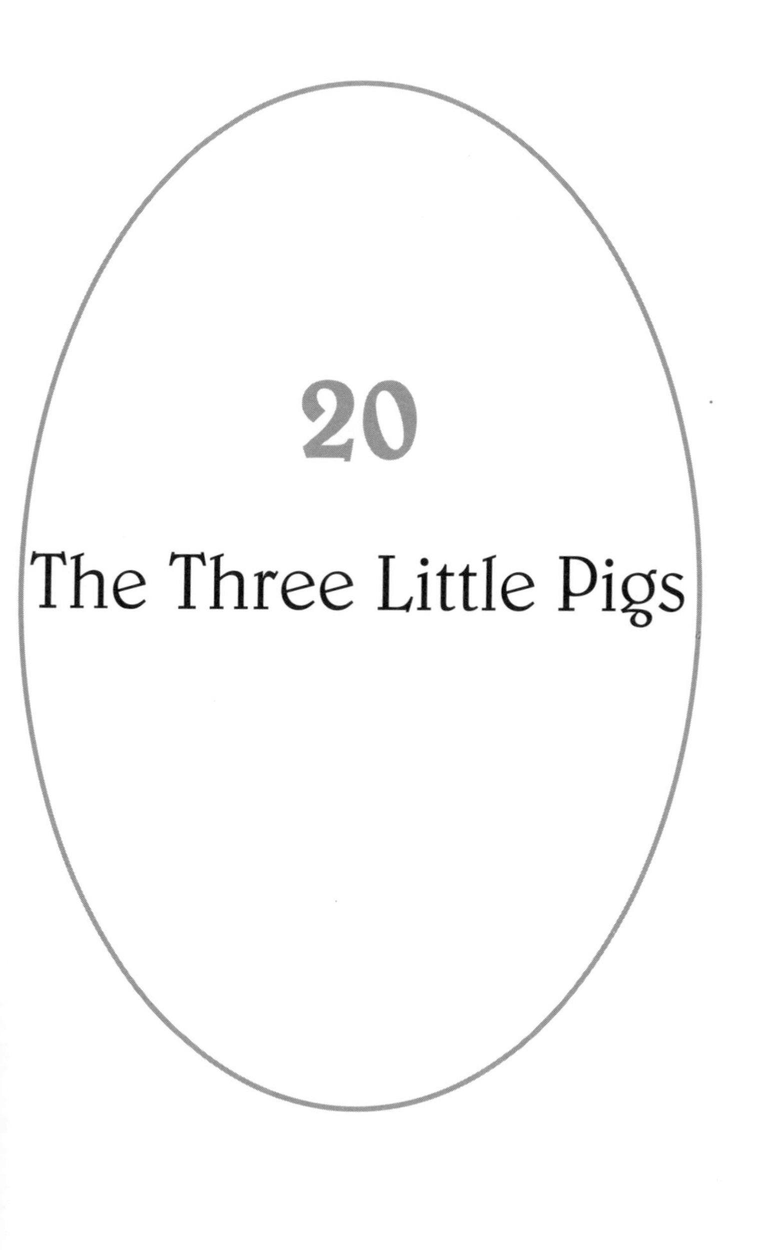

20

The Three Little Pigs

Once upon a time there was a mother pig who had three little pigs. As the little pigs grew up, there were more mouths than the mother pig could feed, so she decided to send the young ones out into the world to make their fortunes.

One fine morning the three little pigs started out into the wide world, each along a different road.

The first little pig walked along in the

wide world until he met a man with a load of straw.

"Please, Mr. Man," said the first little pig, "give me some straw to build me a little house."

The man gave the first little pig some straw, and he built himself a house.

The first little pig was no more than settled in his straw house when a wicked wolf came along.

"Little pig, little pig, let me in, let me in!" he called.

"Not by the hair of my chinny, chin, chin!" answered the first little pig.

"If you don't," said the wolf, "I'll huff and I'll puff and I'll blow your house in!"

But the first little pig wouldn't.

So the wolf huffed

and he puffed

and he blew the house in,

and he ate up the first little pig.

Now the second little pig walked along in the wide world until he met a man with a load of sticks.

"Please, Mr. Man," said the second little pig, "give me some sticks to build me a little house."

The man gave the second little pig some sticks, and he built himself a house.

The second little pig was no more than settled in his house of sticks when along came the wicked wolf.

"Little pig, little pig, let me in, let me in!" he called.

"Not by the hair of my chinny, chin, chin!" answered the second little pig.

"If you don't," said the wolf, "I'll huff and I'll puff and I'll blow your house in!"

But the second little pig wouldn't.

So the wolf huffed

and he puffed

and he blew the house in,

and he ate up the second little pig.

Now the third little pig walked along in the wide world until he met a man with a load of bricks.

"Please, Mr. Man," said the third little

pig, "give me some bricks to build me a little house."

The man gave the third little pig some bricks, and he built himself a house.

The third little pig was no more than settled in his house of bricks when along came the wolf.

"Little pig, little pig, let me in, let me in!" he called.

"Not by the hair of my chinny, chin, chin!" answered the third little pig.

"If you don't," said the wolf, "I'll huff and I'll puff and I'll blow your house in!"

But the third little pig wouldn't.

So the wolf huffed
and he puffed,
and he puffed
and he huffed,
but he couldn't blow the house in.

Then the wicked wolf slunk off, muttering to himself, "Little pig, little pig, I'll catch you yet!" Soon he was back at the little pig's door.

"Little pig," he called in his friendliest voice, "if you will meet me in Farmer Brown's garden at six o'clock tomorrow morning I will show you where the finest turnips grow."

The next morning the little pig got up at five o'clock and hurried to Farmer Brown's garden. By the time the wolf came at six, the little pig was safe and snug at home again, with his turnips on the stove.

So the wicked wolf slunk off, muttering to himself, "Little pig, little pig, I'll catch you yet." Soon he was back at the little pig's door.

"Little pig," he called in his friendliest voice, "if you will meet me in Farmer Brown's orchard at five o'clock tomorrow morning I will show you where the finest apples are."

The next morning the little pig got up at four o'clock and hurried to Farmer Brown's orchard. But he was still up in an apple tree when he saw the wolf coming, down below.

"Ah, so you have found the apples, little pig," grinned the wolf, thinking he had trapped the little pig at last.

"Yes, won't you try one?" said the little pig, and he threw down a big red apple to the wolf.

But he threw it so hard that it rolled down a big hill and the wolf had to go running after it. While the wolf was running, the little pig scrambled down and ran home with his basket full.

When the wolf found he had been fooled he slunk off, muttering to himself, "Little pig, little pig, I'll catch you yet." Soon he was back at the little pig's door.

"Little pig," he called, still in his friendliest voice, "tomorrow there is a fair in the village. If you will meet me there at three o'clock I will show you the best bargains."

The next day the little pig got to the fair at two o'clock and bought himself a new butter churn. He was just starting home with it when he saw the wolf coming up the road.

The little pig had nowhere else to hide so he jumped into the churn, and away he went, rolling down the hill toward the wolf.

The wolf was so frightened that he ran as fast as he could go.

The little pig in his churn rolled straight on home.

When the wolf found he had been fooled again he slunk off, muttering worse than ever, "Little pig, little pig, I'll catch you this time." So he climbed up on the little pig's roof and called down the chimney, "Now, little pig, I am coming down to eat you up."

"Oh, are you?" the little pig called back, and he took the lid off a huge pot of water bubbling on the fire, just as the wolf jumped down the chimney.

Down tumbled the wolf right into the boiling water. Then the little pig popped the cover back onto the pot, and that was the end of the wolf.

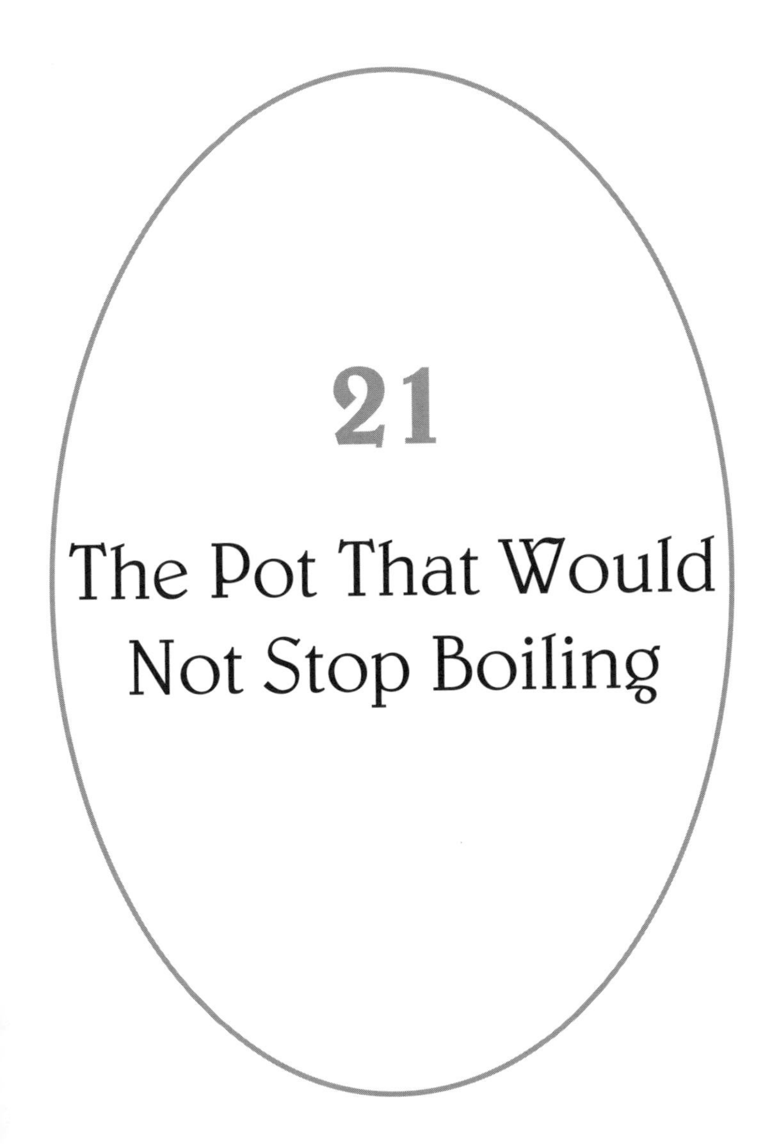

21

The Pot That Would Not Stop Boiling

There was once a little girl who lived with her mother in a tiny little house. They were very, very poor, and often did not even have enough to eat.

One day there was nothing at all in the house to eat, so the mother sent the little girl out into the woods to hunt for berries. As the little girl wandered in the woods she met an old woman.

"Why are you out in the woods alone,

my dear?" asked the old woman. When the little girl told her, the old woman pulled out from under her heavy cloak a little iron pot.

"This is a magic pot, my dear," said the little old woman. "Whenever you are hungry, just say to it, 'Cook, little pot, cook!' and you will have sweet porridge. When you have enough, all you need to say is, 'Stop, little pot, stop!' and it will stop."

The little girl thanked the old woman and ran all the way home with the little magic pot.

From that time on the little girl and her mother never went hungry, for whenever they needed food, the little girl would say:

"Cook, little pot, cook!" and the little pot would fill up with sweet porridge.

Then the little girl would say:

"Stop, little pot, stop!" and the little pot would stop boiling.

But one day when the little girl was away from home, her mother got hungry for some good sweet porridge. So she took out the little pot and said:

"Cook, little pot, cook!"

Soon the little pot was full of sweet porridge.

"No more, little pot, no more!" said the mother. But the porridge climbed up to the brim of the little pot and began to spill over the edges.

"Halt, little pot, halt!" cried the mother. But the porridge kept coming. It ran over the stove and began to drip onto the floor.

Try as she might, the mother could not think of the right words to make the little pot stop boiling. So the porridge spread out over the kitchen floor, and grew deeper and deeper.

It ran out the door and trickled down the path. Soon the trickle was a stream that went rushing down the little village street, pushing its way into houses. And still the little pot kept on boiling.

The stream of porridge flowed along, growing deeper and faster, until it came to the last house in the village, where the little girl was visiting. When she saw the first trickle of porridge creep in under the door, she guessed what had happened, and she ran home through the porridge-filled streets.

"Stop, little pot, stop!" cried the little girl as she waded into the kitchen.

Instantly the little pot stopped boiling. But by that time the village was so full of porridge that it took the people three weeks to eat their way out of it.

Turn the page for
more stories.

22

The Goose That Laid the Golden Egg

There once lived a man who owned a wonderful goose. Each day he went to the barnyard and said to the goose: "Where is my golden egg?"

And every day the goose laid one shining golden egg. Then the man took the egg to market and sold it for a great deal of money. And he and his family lived in comfort.

But one day a neighbor said to the man:

"Why are you satisfied with one egg a day? Surely that goose must be lined with gold. Why not cut it open and get all the gold?"

At first the man could not bring himself to kill the bird which had brought him such comfort. But at length his greed got the better of him. So he went to the barnyard and killed the goose that laid the golden eggs.

Quickly he cut it open—and found just what you would find if you cut open an ordinary, every-day goose.

Now there were no more golden eggs each morning, and the greedy farmer and his family had to work hard for their living the rest of their days.